ISADORA MOON

Goes Camping

Harriet Muncaster

A STEPPING STONE BOOK™
Random House New York

For vampires, fairies, and humans everywhere!
And for Erin Green, dolphin queen.

 Published in the United States by Random House Children's Books, a division of Penguin Random House LLC, New York. Originally published in paperback by Oxford University Press, Oxford, in 2016.

Random House and the colophon are registered trademarks and A Stepping Stone Book and the colophon are trademarks of Penguin Random House LLC.

Visit us on the Web!
SteppingStonesBooks.com
randomhousekids.com

Educators and librarians, for a variety of teaching tools, visit us at RHTeachersLibrarians.com

Library of Congress Cataloging-in-Publication Data is available upon request.
ISBN 978-0-399-55825-2 (hc) — ISBN 978-0-399-55826-9 (lib. bdg.) — ISBN 978-0-399-55827-6 (pbk.) — ISBN 978-0-399-55828-3 (ebook)

MANUFACTURED IN CHINA
10 9 8 7 6
First American Edition

This book has been officially leveled by using the F&P Text Level Gradient™ Leveling System.

ISADORA MOON

Goes Camping

Chapter One

Isadora Moon, that's me! And my best friend is Pink Rabbit. He was my favorite toy, so Mom brought him to life with her magic wand. Mom can do things like that because she is a fairy. Oh, and did I also mention that my dad is a vampire? That makes me half-fairy, half-vampire!

My second-best friends are Zoe and Oliver. We all go to the same school together. It's a regular school for human children. I love it!

Every morning Zoe and Oliver pick me up, and we walk to school together. Mom and Dad always try to avoid opening the door. They are still a bit funny about talking to humans.

It was the first day back at school after the summer break, and I was really looking forward to seeing my friends. As soon as I heard a "bang bang bang" on the door, I flew to open it.

"Zoe!" I said, leaping on top of her and

giving her a big hug. I didn't leap on top of Oliver because he doesn't like hugs.

We started to walk down the sidewalk together, and Pink Rabbit bounced along beside us. Zoe made a tinkling sound as

she walked, because she was wearing a lot of jewelry. She wants to be an actress when she grows up and is always dressing up as different people.

"Today I am the queen!" she told me, twizzling one of her necklaces around her finger and patting the paper crown on her head. "Queen Zoe!"

"I like your bracelets," I said. "Where did you get them?"

"In France!" said Zoe. "That's where we went over the summer. It was *très* fantastic. We got to ride on a ferry boat."

"Ooh, that sounds great," said Oliver. He loves boats.

Then Zoe looked in her bag and pulled out another bracelet.

"This one's for you, Isadora," she said. "From France."

"Wow!" I said, taking the bracelet. "Thanks, Zoe!" I felt all glowy inside as I put it on.

"And this is for you, Oliver," said Zoe, holding out a magnet in the shape of the French flag.

"Cool!" said Oliver. "Thanks, Zoe."

It was very kind of Zoe to bring me something from her vacation, but I felt a tiny bit embarrassed that I hadn't got anything for her.

"I can't wait for show-and-tell today," said Oliver. "I've brought photos of my trip. We stayed in a hotel by the beach!"

"That sounds nice," I said, and then I tried to change the subject. I suddenly didn't want to talk about vacations anymore. Especially *my* vacation. I had been to the beach, like Zoe and Oliver, but strange things had happened there . . . the sorts of things that probably didn't happen on human vacations.

When we got to school, our teacher, Miss Cherry, was already arranging the classroom for show-and-tell.

"Good morning, everyone!" she said, beaming around the classroom. "I hope you all had a wonderful summer. Who wants to

SHOW
+
TELL

come up and talk about their summer break first?"

A lot of hands shot up into the air, and I tried to slink down behind my desk. I really didn't want to stand up and tell everyone about my vacation. I was sure they would all think my summer break was not normal. I felt embarrassed.

"Isadora Moon!" said Miss Cherry. "How about you?"

I stared at her in panic.

"Come on," she said. "I'm sure you had a lovely summer."

Slowly, I stood up and walked to the front of the class. A sea of expectant faces stared back at me. I took a deep breath and felt my voice wobble.

"Well . . . ," I began.

Chapter Two

It all started one sunny morning. I came downstairs to find Mom waving her wand around in the kitchen. She had made a flower-patterned tent appear, and it was sitting in the middle of the floor. My baby sister, Honeyblossom, was in her high chair smashing toast in her face, and Dad was sitting at the table with her, yawning (he had just come back from his nightly fly) and drinking his red juice. Dad only ever drinks red juice. It's a vampire thing.

Mom smiled at me as I came into the room. "There you are!" she said. "What do you think of this?" She pointed at the tent. "Do you like the pattern? It's for you. We're going camping!"

"WHAT?!" said Dad.

"Camping!" Mom repeated. "We're going camping at the beach. I booked it this morning."

"I," said Dad primly, "do not *do* camping."

"Oh, don't be silly!" said Mom. "You'll love it! There's nothing better than waking up outdoors with the morning sunshine blasting into your tent . . . cooking on a campfire . . . playing in the sand. It's wonderful to be so close to nature!"

Dad did not look convinced.

I walked around the tent in the middle of the floor, inspecting it and lifting the flap to peer inside.

"So what do you think?" Mom asked again.

"I'm not sure about the color," I admitted. "It's a bit *too* pink and flowery. . . ."

"Okay," said Mom. "How about this?" She waved her wand again, and the tent changed to a black-and-white-striped pattern.

"Ooh, yes, that's more like it," I said,

crawling inside. Pink Rabbit followed me, and we sat crouched under the canvas walls listening to Mom and Dad.

"We'll be right next to the beach, so we can go swimming in the ocean every day," Mom was saying. Pink Rabbit put his paws over his ears. He hates getting wet, because it takes him ages to dry. We have to pin him up outside on the clothesline.

"And anyway," Mom said, "it's booked. It's final. We're going camping. We leave this afternoon. So you'd better get packing!"

"Well," said Dad, "I'm going up to take a bath and enjoy the comforts of home while I still can."

I wondered how Dad was going to cope

Gel

without his bathroom on our camping trip. He does like to spend a lot of time in there. He has baths that last for hours while he plays classical music and lights hundreds of flickering candles. Then he spends at least an hour with his special comb, smoothing down his shiny black hair with gel.

"A vampire's hair is their pride and joy," he always says. "You should brush yours more often."

After breakfast, we all went to pack our things and then stood by the front door, waiting for Dad. Eventually, he appeared at the top of the stairs with five giant suitcases.

"You can't bring all that!" Mom gasped.

Toothpaste
SoAP

"It won't fit in the car!"

"We will strap it on to the roof, then," Dad said cheerfully.

Mom sighed. She tried to pick up one of the suitcases, but it was so heavy she couldn't even get it off the ground.

"What *have* you got in there?" she said, waving her wand at it. The suitcase sprang open, and hundreds of Dad's grooming products burst out onto the floor.

Mom rolled her eyes. She pointed at

a twirly black comb. "Surely you're not bringing that," she said. "That's your great-great-great-grandfather's antique jeweled vampire comb."

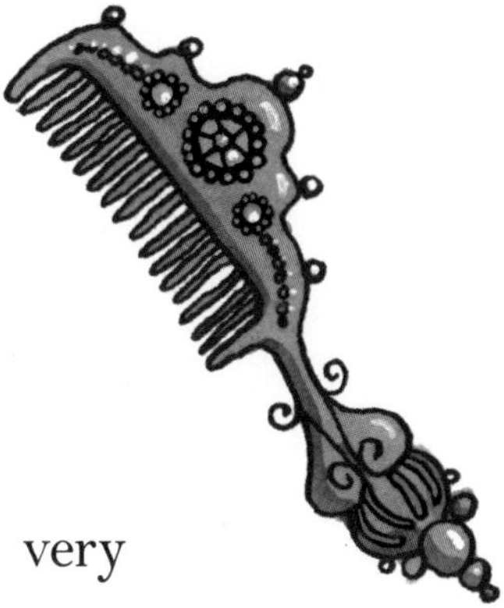

"Yes, and it's my favorite thing!" Dad said.

"But that comb is very precious," said Mom, helping Dad put everything back into the suitcase. "You don't want to lose it."

"I won't lose it," said Dad, picking it up and admiring the red rubies that sparkled in the handle. "Look how it shines."

Dad's suitcases took up so much space

that there was barely room for Pink Rabbit, Honeyblossom, and me to sit in the back. It wasn't very comfortable.

It was a very long drive. Pink Rabbit kept bouncing up and down on my lap, trying to spot the ocean out the window. Bounce, bounce, bounce. And then at last, **BOUNCE!** Because finally there it was. The blue sparkling ocean, like a glittering ribbon across the horizon.

"THE BEACH!" I shouted. "There's the ocean! We're here!"

Honeyblossom waved her chubby little arms in approval.

Mom started humming as she drove the car down a bumpy countryside lane. Pink Rabbit and I stared out the window. At the end of the lane there was a sign. It read:

"That's us!" said Mom cheerfully, driving past the sign and into a small field with lots of tents.

"Isn't it just beautiful!" said Mom as we parked and got out of the car. "Breathe in that fresh ocean air, Isadora!"

I took a long sniff. So did Pink Rabbit. It smelled salty and fresh.

Mom used magic to set up the tents. The one Mom, Dad, and Honeyblossom were sharing was really huge. And not *usual*-looking.

"You can always come into our tent if you get scared in the night," said Mom.

"I won't be scared!" I laughed. "I am half-vampire. I love the night!"

Dad was busy going through his suitcases. "I know I put that bat-patterned wallpaper somewhere," he muttered. "And in which suitcase did I put my pop-up four-poster bed? And where on earth am I supposed to plug in my portable fridge?"

By the time we were all unpacked, it was dark. Mom and I made a campfire, and we all sat around it toasting marshmallows on long sticks.

"Isn't this wonderful?" said Mom. "This is what camping is all about!"

I nodded. My mouth was full of gooey marshmallow.

Even Dad seemed to have perked up a bit since the sun had gone down. He sucked on the straw of his carton of red juice and stared up at the sky.

"You can see more stars now that we're in the countryside," said Dad. He leapt up to go and find his special astronomer's telescope from their tent.

"I'm going to stargaze all night!" he said happily.

"Not all night," said Mom. "You need to get some sleep so we can have a day at the beach tomorrow."

"But vampires are awake at night and sleep in the day! It's what we do," he gasped.

"Just try it," said Mom.

Dad sighed.

"I'll try," he promised.

Chapter Three

When you are camping, you have to walk to a place called The Outhouse in your pajamas to brush your teeth and take a shower. I had to brush my teeth at a sink next to other people staying at the campsite. It felt a bit funny wearing my pajamas in public, but it didn't matter because everyone else was wearing them too!

We had to use Mom's wand as a flashlight to walk back across the field after brushing our teeth. Then Pink Rabbit and I crawled into our striped tent and snuggled under

our sleeping bags. It was very cozy. Dad zipped the door up tight for us.

"Good night, Isadora," he said. "Good night, Pink Rabbit."

I yawned. "Good night."

Then I lay there in the dark for a bit. There were strange noises all around. Things rustling, owls hooting, people talking. But I wasn't scared. I love the dark!

I woke up early the next morning because the sun was shining brightly on the roof of my tent. It was very hot.

"Good morning," Mom chirped when I poked my head outside. "We're going to the beach as soon as you're ready. We just need to find Dad first. He's disappeared somewhere. . . ."

I had an idea of where Dad might be.

Outside the one shower cubicle in The Outhouse was a long line of grumbling people. I skipped past all of them and knocked on the door.

"Dad?" I said.

"Yes?"

"How long have you been in there?"

"Only a couple of hours."

A cloud of warm steam rose up from under the door, and Dad started humming contentedly.

"Dad," I said again. "There's a long line of people waiting, you know."

"Is there?" said Dad, sounding surprised.

"*Yes,*" I said. "You need to hurry up. We're going to the beach."

I heard the shower turn off.

"All right," he said. "I'm coming." Dad appeared in his towel. He looked very refreshed.

We walked back along the line of people, and I felt my cheeks turn pink with embarrassment. They were all staring at Dad, and they didn't look very happy.

"There you are!" said Mom when we got back to the tent. "Now we can go to the beach!"

"I'm not ready *yet,*" said Dad. "Just give me five minutes."

Half an hour later, Dad emerged from the tent, wearing his black cape and sunglasses and holding a black umbrella tucked under his arm. He was also holding a jar of hair gel and his great-great-great-grandfather's precious antique vampire comb.

"I'm ready!" Dad grinned.

Chapter Four

We went through a little gate at the edge of the campsite and walked down a sandy path to the beach. Mom spread out a picnic blanket and sat down.

"Isn't it wonderful!" she said.

It was pretty wonderful. The ocean was

blue and sparkly, and the sand was warm and tickly between my toes.

"Come and build a sand castle with me, Dad!" I said.

"Okay! Just give me five minutes," Dad said. He put up his big black umbrella and slathered himself with sunscreen. Then he wrapped himself in his black cape and got out his comb.

"You must be hot, Dad," I said to him as I started building a sand castle nearby.

Dad shook his head.

"I am not hot," he insisted as sweat began to drip down his face. He started to do his hair, smoothing big gloops of gel into it.

By the time Dad was done combing and smoothing his hair, I had finished building my sand castle. It was a very big one with lots of towers. Pink Rabbit and I walked along the beach, collecting shells. We poked them into the castle walls for decoration.

"It needs something else," I said to Pink Rabbit once we had placed all the shells. "It needs something on the top to just finish it off."

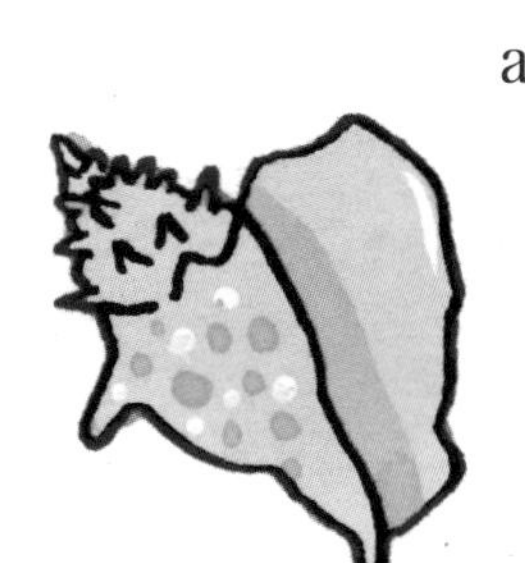

I glanced over to where Dad was now snoozing under the umbrella, and an idea crept into my head.

"Dad won't notice if we borrow the jeweled comb for just ten minutes," I whispered to Pink Rabbit. We tiptoed over, and I picked up the comb. It really was very

beautiful. The rubies in the handle flashed in the sunlight. I pressed it down into the very top of the highest castle tower and stood back to admire my handiwork.

I glanced at Dad, but he was still asleep.

"Isadora," Mom called over. "Do you want to go in the water with me and Honeyblossom?"

"Yes, please!" I shouted excitedly.

So we put Honeyblossom in her floaty and went down to the shore.

"Come on, Dad!" I called. "It's nice and cool in the water!"

But Dad was still asleep under the umbrella and didn't hear me. I thought it was a shame. I know Dad enjoys swimming. He is the one who takes me to my Little Vampires swimming lessons every week. We always have lots of fun in the pool together. He has been trying to teach me to swim underwater, but I haven't managed it yet.

“This is nice!” said Mom, splashing around in the water with Honeyblossom.

Honeyblossom waved her little arms and kicked her little feet. She opened her mouth and squealed with happiness . . .

. . . and her pacifier dropped into the water.

“Oh no!” said Mom, trying to catch it.

I watched as the pacifier began to sink slowly down to the bottom of the sea. Honeyblossom started to wail.

“Oh no!” said Mom again.

“WAAAAAAHH!” screamed Honeyblossom.

I decided I would be brave. I held my breath and scrunched up my eyes, and then I put my head *under the water*!

All I could hear was the roar of the waves, and when I peeped my eyes open, everything was hazy and green. I pushed my arms out in front of me and reached for the pacifier.

"Isadora!" shouted Mom in an excited voice when I popped my head back up a few seconds later. "You just swam underwater!"

I held the pacifier up in the air like a trophy.

"I did it!" I yelled.

"Well done," said Mom, smiling proudly. "That's a real achievement!"

"I wish Dad had seen it," I said.

By the time we got out of the water, the

tide had come in and my sand castle had disappeared under the water. Dad was busy packing away all our things.

"I'm sure I brought it," he muttered.

"What have you lost?" Mom asked.

"My comb!" replied Dad. "My great-great-great-grandfather's precious antique vampire comb!"

I froze. Suddenly, my whole body felt cold even though it was a warm day. I stared at the spot where my sand castle had been. I

had forgotten to take Dad's comb off the top of my castle, and now it had been washed away!

"Dad . . . ," I began. But the words wouldn't come out of my mouth.

"I'm sure I had it," Dad was saying, scratching his head in confusion. "It was right **HERE**."

"It can't have gone far," Mom said as she started to poke around in the sand where Dad had been sitting.

"It's been stolen!" Dad howled.

"Nonsense," said Mom. "Who on earth could have stolen it?"

"A crab?" Dad sniffed. "A sneaky little crab!"

"That's not *very* likely," said Mom. "It must be somewhere around here. Let me try a spell."

She waved her wand, but the comb did not appear.

"That's funny." Mom frowned. "My magic usually works."

I felt so guilty that my stomach hurt, but I couldn't seem to get the words out of my mouth to tell Dad that his comb was lost. . . .

We all walked back up the beach toward the campsite. Dad's mouth was turned down at the edges. He did not look happy.

"We will have to tell him soon," I whispered to Pink Rabbit. "Maybe after dinner, at bedtime. He might be more cheerful when he's had his red juice."

Pink Rabbit nodded. He knows it is best to always be honest.

When Dad came to tuck us in at bedtime, I blurted out, "I'm really sorry about your comb, Dad."

"It's not your fault, Isadora." He smiled sadly. "I'm sure it will turn up."

I took a deep breath.

"Actually . . . ," I began. But Dad had turned his head because Mom was calling him.

"I'd better go," he said. "Good night, Isadora."

"Good night," I whispered.

Chapter Five

Pink Rabbit and I lay in the dark. I felt so bad about the comb that I couldn't sleep.

It was lost forever at the bottom of the deep blue sea!

Or was it?

I sat up in bed. Was there a chance that

the comb had washed back up on the sand?

I scrambled out from under my sleeping bag and crawled toward the opening of our tent.

"Pink Rabbit!" I whispered. "Wake up! We're going to the beach."

Pink Rabbit bounced out of bed. I don't think he had been able to sleep either. Together we crept out of the tent and stood in the dark field. The sky was full of stars, and all we could hear were the faint sounds of people snoring.

I tiptoed over to Mom and Dad's tent.

"We'll need Mom's wand for a flashlight," I whispered to Pink Rabbit.

I silently slid the wand out of Mom's bag. I waved it in the air, and the star immediately glowed pink. I reached down for Pink Rabbit's paw, and together we flapped up into the air.

I love to fly, especially at night. We soared high over the field until all the tents were just little black specks. Then we swooped down toward the beach and the sound of the roaring waves.

I pointed Mom's wand down at the sand.

"It might have washed up around here," I said hopefully.

We walked back and forth along the shoreline, squinting in the pink wand light. Little bits of sea glass and pearly shells winked up at us, but none of them were Dad's comb. Pink Rabbit held on to my hand tightly. He finds the darkness a bit too mysterious sometimes.

Suddenly, there came a small splashing sound from the sea.

I stared at Pink Rabbit.

"What was that?" I whispered.

Pink Rabbit didn't know, because he had his paws over his eyes.

I peered out to sea. There was something shining and sparkling in the water. Maybe it was Dad's comb! I rose up into the air, pulling Pink Rabbit behind me.

"Come on!" I said to him. "Let's look!"

We fluttered toward the shining thing in the sea. As we got closer I could see that it was moving. “It can’t be the comb,” I said to Pink Rabbit. We flew a little closer and heard a soft tinkly voice calling out.

“Hello?”

I could see that there was a girl about my age in the sea. She had long, long hair and a gleaming fish tail that kept flicking in and out of the water. I hovered above her, holding Pink Rabbit clear of the waves.

“Are you a mermaid?” I asked.

“Yes,” she said in a songlike voice. “How are you floating up there?”

“I’m flying, not floating! I am half-fairy,

half-vampire." I turned in the air to show her my wings.

"I've never met a half-fairy, half-vampire before!" she said.

"I've never met a mermaid before!" I replied.

We both laughed. She had a laugh that sounded like strings of shells tinkling in the breeze.

"My name's Marina. What's yours?"

"Isadora," I said. Then I pointed at Pink Rabbit. "This is Pink Rabbit."

"He's funny." She giggled, reaching out and poking his stomach.

Pink Rabbit stiffened. He doesn't like to be called funny.

"What are you doing out here so late at night?" Marina asked.

"I was looking for something really precious. It got lost here today while we were at the beach."

"Oh?" Marina said. "What is it?"

"A comb," I said. "A really special comb. It's my dad's."

"Was it black?" Marina asked. "With twirly designs on it? And rubies?"

"Yes!" I said hopefully. "Have you seen it?!"

"I have . . . ," said Marina, "but . . ."

"Where is it?" I asked excitedly. "I need it back!"

Marina looked a bit worried.

"The Mermaid Princess has it," she said.

"All the nicest jewels found on the beach always go to the Mermaid Princess. She doesn't like to share."

"But it's my dad's comb," I said in a panicky voice. "I need it back." I felt my eyes fill with tears.

Marina bit her lip. "It's tricky," she said. "There are different rules for under the sea, you know. It's finders keepers here."

I wiped my eyes and sniffed.

"I'll tell you what," said Marina. "Why don't I take you to the Mermaid Princess? You can ask her yourself! Maybe she'll let you have it back if you explain."

I felt Pink Rabbit tug at my hand in fright. He hates the water.

"It's not far to the palace," said Marina. "Just follow me. Come on!"

I stared at the water, now black under the night sky.

"I *can* swim underwater now," I told Marina proudly. "But I can't hold my breath for very long. How can we follow you?"

Marina laughed her tinkly laugh again.

"Silly me!" she said. "I forgot! Wear this so you can breathe underwater. It's magical." She handed me a necklace made of shells, and I put it on.

“What about Pink Rabbit? He hates getting wet.”

“Hmm,” Marina said, thinking hard. “I know!” She splashed her tail in the water to make some bubbles on the surface, and then she lifted one of the bubbles out of the water on the tip of her finger and blew on it. It got bigger and bigger until it was big

enough for Pink Rabbit to hop inside. Then she held out her hand to me.

"Come on," she said. "Let's go."

I smiled, trying to show I was not afraid, and let her pull me down toward the water. It was cold at first, and I gasped.

"You'll get used to it," Marina said.

Chapter Six

Everything under the water gleamed in the moonlight. The seaweed swayed gently below us, and little silver fishes darted in and out. I was surprised to find that I could breathe as easily as if I were on land. I glanced back over my shoulder to check that Pink Rabbit was all right in his bubble.

Marina pointed to a silhouette in the distance.

"There's the palace," she said. "It's not far at all!"

"You can speak underwater!" I said in surprise. And then I put my hand to my mouth. "So can I!" I said in wonder.

Marina laughed again.

“That’s because you’re wearing the magic necklace,” she explained. “And of course I can speak underwater—I’m a mermaid!”

We swam on toward the silhouette. Now it was getting closer, and I could make out spires and towers looming up toward the surface of the water. It was very pretty, with shells stuck all around the walls, just like my sand castle!

"Here we are," said Marina. She heaved open the gigantic front door and invited me into a large entrance hall lit by twinkly lights. Even the walls were studded with shiny jewels and pearls.

"Wow!" I said, gazing around. "It's so beautiful!"

Marina led us to another big room, with a throne in the middle. And on the throne sat the Mermaid Princess. I could tell she was the princess, because she was wearing a crown. On her lap was a teddy bear, but

instead of legs, it had a fish tail like a mermaid's. The princess was busy combing its fur . . . with Dad's great-great-great-grandfather's special comb!

The princess looked up when we swam into the room. Everything about her sparkled. She had pearls and starfish in her hair, and rows of jeweled bracelets on her arms. Around her neck pearl necklaces shimmered and glimmered in the undersea light.

Marina gave a small cough. "Your Highness," she said, "I have brought someone to see you."

"What is this?" the princess said, sounding puzzled. "You don't have a tail!"

"No," I said. "But I do have wings! I am a vampire-fairy. I'm Isadora Moon, and this is Pink Rabbit."

"I see," said the princess, glancing interestedly at Pink Rabbit. "My name is Delphina. *Princess* Delphina. One day I shall be Queen of the Sea!"

I smiled nervously.

"There was actually something I wanted to talk to you about," I said. "That comb you're holding—I was wondering if I could please have it back? I lost it today on the beach. It's my dad's, and it's his very special favorite thing. He's very upset about losing it."

Princess Delphina's eyes glittered with tears.

"But I like it. It's so sparkly." She held it

up in the water so that the rubies flashed in the glowing lights.

"Yes, but it's not really yours to keep," I said.

"Well, I suppose you can have the comb back . . . if you stay for the tea party."

"Oh," I said, surprised. "Okay. Of course we will stay for the tea party!"

Chapter Seven

So Pink Rabbit and Marina and I had a tea party with Princess Delphina and her mer-bear. We had cupcakes and sea berries and little shrimp sandwiches with the crusts cut off. It was all very nice, but everything tasted a little soggy.

"That was lovely," I said politely. "Thank

you. Could I please have the comb now?"

Princess Delphina frowned.

"I will give it to you . . . if you play a game of hide-and-seek with me," she said.

"But—" I began.

"I'll count!" said the princess. "Go and hide!"

So we all played hide-and-seek for a long time, and Marina whispered to me that we must always let the princess win. So we did.

"That was great fun!" said the princess. "Let's play something else now!"

I stared up toward the surface of the water and felt worried. It was starting to get light.

"Let's play . . . dress-up!" said the Mermaid Princess, and she led us over to a big box of jewels by her throne. She began to pick out pearl necklaces and coral bracelets and shiny tiaras made of shells and starfish.

"Put these on!" she ordered, holding the jewels out toward me.

"I . . . ," I started to object.

"Oh, go on," the princess said. "No one ever comes to play with me."

I glanced up at the surface of the water again. It was getting lighter by the second.

"I can't," I said. "I'm sorry, but I really have to go. Can I have the comb back now, please?"

The princess looked annoyed and a little bit sad.

"I'll give it to you . . . if you give me Pink Rabbit," she said.

"Oh no!" I said, shocked. "I absolutely cannot give you Pink Rabbit. And he would hate living under the sea."

The princess looked disappointed, and suddenly I knew what was the matter. She was lonely.

"I have an idea," I said. "Why don't I try to bring your mer-bear to life for you in exchange for the comb? I have my mom's wand with me. I think I know how to do it."

The princess's eyes lit up. She hugged her mer-bear to her chest and then held it out toward me.

"Yes!" she said. "Yes! If you can make my bear come alive, I promise I will give you the comb."

I held out Mom's wand and pointed it at the bear. Using a magic wand is not my strongest skill, but I had to try. I waved it back and forth in the water, and a stream of bubbles shot out of the end. When they cleared, the mer-bear was twitching his head and moving his paw around.

But still, something wasn't quite right. . . .

Quickly, I waved the wand again. . . .

And again. . . .

Until finally . . . I got it right.

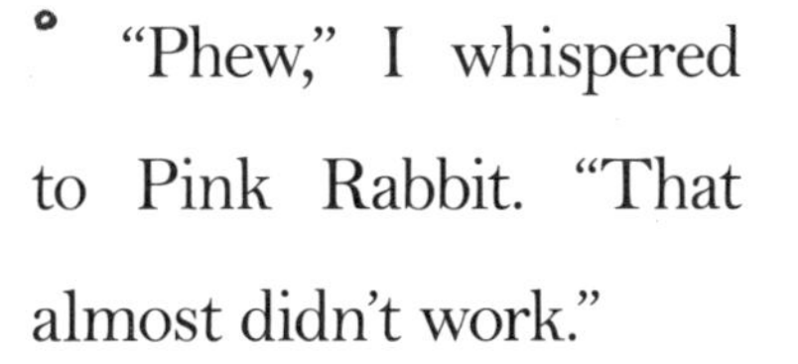

"Phew," I whispered to Pink Rabbit. "That almost didn't work."

The princess beamed happily as her mer-bear swam around her head in circles.

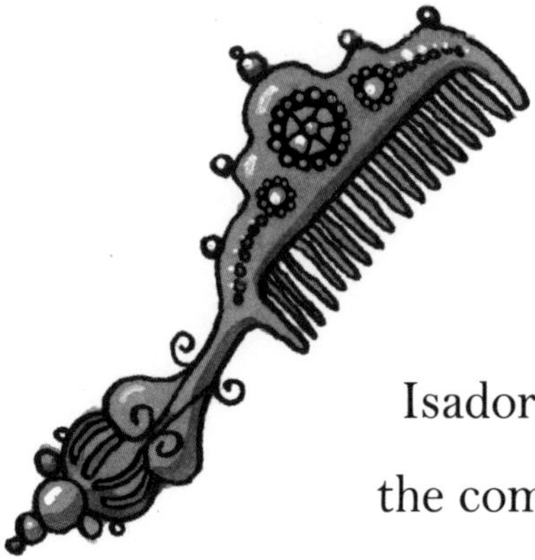

She held out the comb to me.

"Thank you, Isadora!" she said. "Take the comb. It's yours!"

I tucked the comb safely in my pajama pocket before the princess could change her mind, and then Marina and I said goodbye and left the palace.

As we swam back up toward the surface, I could see it was morning.

We came out of the water, and I took a big gulp of air. Pink Rabbit's bubble popped, and I caught him just before he fell.

Marina smiled at me, and I smiled back.

"It was nice to meet you," she said.

"It was nice to meet you too," I replied. "Thank you so much for helping me find my dad's comb."

"It was a pleasure," said Marina in her tinkly little voice. "And you've made the Mermaid Princess very happy."

I started to take the magic necklace off.

"Keep it," said Marina. "It won't work again, but it's pretty. You can wear it!"

"Thank you," I said, feeling very happy inside.

Marina glanced at the rising sun.

"I'd better go," she said. "I don't want to be spotted by any humans. And you'd better get back too."

I nodded and flapped my wings, sending

a flurry of water droplets flying as I rose into the air.

"Goodbye, Marina!" I said.

"Goodbye, Isadora!" she replied. And then with a splash and a laugh, she was gone.

I held Pink Rabbit in my arms, and we flew as fast as we could back to the campsite. It was still very early, and all was quiet. I snuck into Mom and Dad's tent and slipped the wand into Mom's bag before heading to my own tent to put on some dry clothes. When I poked my head out of my tent again, I got the surprise of my life.

Dad was sitting by the campfire! He was wearing a T-shirt and shorts, and he was busy making breakfast for everyone.

"There you are, Isadora," he said. "You're up bright and early!"

"But . . . but . . . what are you doing up so early?" I asked.

"It looks like it's going to be a lovely day," said Dad. "We're going to the beach

again. Last night, Mom told me that you swam underwater yesterday. I'm really sorry I missed it. It made me realize that I don't want to miss out on anything else this vacation. I can't wait for you to show me your underwater swimming later!"

"I can't wait to show you!" I said. "But what about your comb, Dad?"

He looked sad for a minute, but then he shook his head and shrugged.

"It was a beautiful comb," he said. "And very precious. But it was my own fault for bringing it to the beach. I should have left it in the tent. And you know, I've been thinking: spending time with my family is more important than a silly comb. Besides," he said, running a hand through his sleek hair, "I've still got my hair gel."

I took the comb from behind my back and held it out to Dad. His eyes went big and wide, and his mouth made an O shape.

"I'm really sorry," I said, "but it was me who lost your comb. I put it on my sand castle, and the sea washed it away. But then I went and searched for it and found it! I'm sorry I didn't tell you sooner."

Dad took the comb, and his face creased up with delight.

"My comb!" he cried, jumping into the air. "My beloved comb!" He kissed it and ran away into his tent to lock it safely in his suitcase.

When Dad came back, we sat down together next to the campfire.

"You know, Isadora," Dad said, "I'm glad you found my comb, but honesty is always

the best policy. If you had told me you'd lost it, we could have looked for it together."

"Sorry, Dad," I said.

Dad gave me a big hug, and we cooked breakfast together.

After that, it was time to go to the beach, and it was the best day ever. Dad came in the water and let me ride on his back, and then I showed him my underwater swimming, which was loads better after all the practice I had the night before. Dad was very impressed. We had a picnic together, and then we made the biggest, fanciest sand castle ever!

"It's fit for a vampire-fairy-mermaid princess!" Dad said.

That night, I felt so happy as we all sat around the campfire and ate our dinner. Dad even tried a roasted marshmallow on a stick! Usually, he refuses anything but red juice.

"Isadora's underwater swimming was fantastic!" he said. "I'm so glad I got to see it today."

I felt prouder than ever as I licked my marshmallow.

Dad put his arms around me and Mom and Honeyblossom, and the firelight flickered on our faces. Suddenly, I felt very tired.

"You were just like a mermaid!" said Dad as I snuggled into him.

I laughed sleepily. "Don't be silly, Dad," I said. "Everyone knows there's no such thing as mermaids!"

Then I turned my head and winked at Pink Rabbit. Moonlight flashed off his button eyes, and I could tell he was winking back.

I finished talking and realized that the whole class was staring at me with their mouths wide open. Even Miss Cherry.

"It sounds like you had an amazing summer, Isadora!" she said.

"I want to see a mermaid!" shouted Zoe.

"I want to toast marshmallows on a campfire!" said Oliver.

"I want to sleep in a tent!" said someone else.

I pulled the shell necklace out from under my uniform.

"This is the necklace the mermaid gave me," I told the class. I took it off and held it up in the air so that the shells tinkled together. It sounded like Marina's laugh.

"Ooh," they all whispered, their eyes big and round like saucers. Zoe's eyes were the biggest of them all. I walked over to her desk and held out the necklace.

"It's for you," I said to her. "A souvenir!"

Zoe beamed.

"How nice," said Miss Cherry. Then she looked at her watch. "My goodness!" she exclaimed. "Look at the time! We will have to continue show-and-tell after lunch.

Thank you, Isadora, for giving us such an interesting account of your vacation."

I smiled. Suddenly, I didn't mind show-and-tell so much anymore.

"I expect your family will be going camping again next year," said Miss Cherry. "As you had such a wonderful time this summer."

"Oh no!" I said. "Dad gets to choose the vacation next year. We're going to the Nighttime Vampire Hotel. It's got a spa!"

Nighttime
Vampire
Hotel
Luxury
Spa

Family Tree

My mom,
Countess Cordelia
Moon

Baby Honeyblossom

My dad,
Count Bartholomew
Moon

Me!
Isadora Moon

Pink Rabbit

Harriet Muncaster, that's me! I'm the author and illustrator of Isadora Moon.

Yes, really! I love anything teeny-tiny, anything starry, and everything glittery.

Sink your fangs into
Isadora Moon's next adventure!

"We are going on a school trip," Miss Cherry said. "To see a show!"

"A show!" said Zoe. "We were just talking about putting on a pretend show!"

"Well, here's your chance to see a real one," said Miss Cherry. "We're going to see the *Alice in Wonderland* ballet!"

I felt my heart start to beat fast. A ballet show! We were going to see a real ballet show!

"You need to take the letter home and get your parents to sign it," said Miss Cherry. "And we also need some parents to volunteer to help on the trip."

"Will there be cookies during intermission?" called out Bruno.

"I expect there will be ice cream," said Miss Cherry.

"I told you," whispered Sashi.

"There will be quite a famous ballerina playing the part of the White Rabbit," continued Miss Cherry. "You might have heard of her if you're interested in ballet. Her name is Tatiana Tutu."

"Tatiana Tutu!" I shouted, jumping up from my chair. The whole class turned around.

"Yes," said Miss Cherry. "You obviously know her name, Isadora."

"I do," I said in a smaller voice, suddenly aware that everyone was staring at me. I sat down quickly, feeling my face go pink with embarrassment.

Pink Rabbit didn't seem embarrassed at all. He did a little hop and wiggled his ears. He was beside himself with excitement that

Tatiana Tutu was going to play the part of the *rabbit.*

As soon as I got home, I showed the letter to Mom.

"You have to sign it!" I said. "Quick! Or I can't go on the school trip."

"Hang on a second," said Mom. "Let me read it, Isadora. It says here that they're in need of parents to volunteer for the trip."

"They are," I said, starting to feel a bit worried. "But not you and Dad."

"Why not?" asked Mom. "We could volunteer! It would be good for us to get a bit more involved with your school activities."

"It's in the daytime," I said. "Dad will be asleep."

"That's true," said Mom. "What a shame!"

I didn't think it was a shame at all. In fact, I felt quite relieved. But when Dad came down for breakfast that evening, he seemed very interested in the trip.

"I will volunteer!" he said enthusiastically. "I will make an exception! Hand me the pen!"

I held the pen behind my back.

"There's really no need for you both to come . . . ," I began.

But Mom swooped in with her wand and put a magic check mark in the "volunteer" box.

"How exciting!" she said.

New friends. New adventures. Find a new series . . . just for you!

FOR THE SPORTS FAN

FOR THE ADVENTURER

FOR THE SUPERSTAR

FOR THE DREAMER

FOR THE ANIMAL LOVER

FOR THE EXPLORER

Illustrations (from left to right) : © Mark Meyers; © Mike Boldt; © Brigette Barrager; © Qin Leng; © Russ Cox; © Wesley Lowe

RandomHouseKids.com